P9-BYE-391

DOVER · THRIFT · EDITIONS

The Misanthrope

MOLIÈRE

DOVER PUBLICATIONS, INC.
New York

DOVER THRIFT EDITIONS

GENERAL EDITOR: STANLEY APPELBAUM
EDITOR OF THIS VOLUME: SHANE WELLER

Performance

This Dover Thrift Edition may be used in its entirety, in adaptation or in any other way for theatrical productions, professional and amateur, in the United States, without fee, permission or acknowledgment. (This may not apply outside of the United States, as copyright conditions may vary.)

Published in Canada by General Publishing Company, Ltd., 30 Lesmill Road, Don Mills, Toronto, Ontario.

This Dover edition, first published in 1992, contains the unabridged text of *The Misanthrope*, based on the translation from the French by Henri van Laun published in Volume III of *The Dramatic Works of Molière*, William Paterson, Edinburgh, 1876.

Manufactured in the United States of America
Dover Publications, Inc., 31 East 2nd Street, Mineola, N.Y. 11501

Library of Congress Cataloging-in-Publication Data

Molière. 1622–1673.
    [Misanthrope. English]
    The misanthrope / Molière.
        p.   cm. — (Dover thrift editions)
    Translation of: The misanthrope.
    ISBN 0-486-27065-3 (pbk.)
    I. Title. II. Series.
[PQ1837.A445 1992]
842'.4—dc20
                                                       91-27835
                                                          CIP

Note

"MOLIÈRE" WAS THE pseudonym of the French actor-manager and dramatist Jean Baptiste Poquelin (1622–1673). Born in Paris and educated at the Jesuit Collège de Clermont, Molière abandoned his studies and the prospect of a court appointment to form the company of the Illustre Théâtre in 1643. The troupe began touring the French provinces in 1645. Although Molière was himself imprisoned twice for debt, his company returned in 1658 to Paris, where, under the patronage of Philippe, duc d'Orléans (the brother of King Louis XIV), it performed regularly at the theater of the Palais-Royal, becoming the Troupe du roi in 1665.

The Misanthrope, which is among the playwright's finest comedies, was first performed in 1666 at the Palais-Royal. In the original production, Molière himself played the role of Alceste, an implacable commentator on contemporary moral and aesthetic standards; Molière's wife, Armande Béjart, played Célimène. Although the originality of the comic vision in The Misanthrope was recognized immediately, the play provoked a mixed response, primarily because neither mocker nor mocked escapes unscathed: while ridiculing the fatuous literary pretentions and moral hypocrisy of the French aristocracy, the play also relishes the propensity for self-delusion that characterizes the intolerant critic of that same society.

Contents

DRAMATIS PERSONAE

ALCESTE, *in love with Célimène*
PHILINTE, *his friend*
ORONTE, *in love with Célimène*
CÉLIMÈNE, *beloved by Alceste*
ÉLIANTE, *her cousin*
ARSINOÉ, *Célimène's friend*
ACASTE
CLITANDRE } *marquises*
BASQUE, *servant to Célimène*
DUBOIS, *servant to Alceste*
A Guard of the Maréchaussée

SCENE: *At Paris, in* CÉLIMÈNE'S *house*

ACT I.

SCENE I.

PHILINTE, ALCESTE.

PHILINTE. What is the matter? What ails you?

ALCESTE. [*Seated*] Leave me, I pray.

PHILINTE. But, once more, tell me what strange whim . . .

ALCESTE. Leave me, I tell you, and get out of my sight.

PHILINTE. But you might at least listen to people, without getting angry.

ALCESTE. I choose to get angry, and I do not choose to listen.

PHILINTE. I do not understand you in these abrupt moods, and although we are friends, I am the first . . .

ALCESTE. [*Rising quickly*] I, your friend? Lay not that flattering unction to your soul. I have until now professed to be so; but after what I have just seen of you, I tell you candidly that I am such no longer; I have no wish to occupy a place in a corrupt heart.

PHILINTE. I am then very much to be blamed from your point of view, Alceste?

ALCESTE. To be blamed? You ought to die from very shame; there is no excuse for such behavior, and every man of honor must be disgusted at it. I see you almost stifle a man with caresses, show him the most ardent affection, and overwhelm him with protestations, offers, and vows of friendship. Your ebullitions of tenderness know no bounds; and when I ask you who that man is, you can scarcely tell me his name; your feelings for him, the moment you have turned your back, suddenly cool; you speak of him most indifferently to me. Zounds! I call it unworthy, base, and infamous, so far to lower one's self as to act contrary to one's own feelings, and if, by some mischance, I had done such a thing, I should hang myself at once out of sheer vexation.

PHILINTE. I do not see that it is a hanging matter at all; and I beg of you

1

not to think it amiss if I ask you to show me some mercy, for I shall not
hang myself, if it be all the same to you.

ALCESTE.   That is a sorry joke.

PHILINTE.   But, seriously, what would you have people do?

ALCESTE.   I would have people be sincere, and that, like men of honor,
no word be spoken that comes not from the heart.

PHILINTE.   When a man comes and embraces you warmly, you must
pay him back in his own coin, respond as best you can to his show of
feeling, and return offer for offer, and vow for vow.

ALCESTE.   Not so. I cannot bear so base a method, which your fashionable people generally affect; there is nothing I detest so much as the
contortions of these great time-and-lip servers, these affable dispensers
of meaningless embraces, these obliging utterers of empty words who
view every one in civilities, and treat the man of worth and the fop
alike. What good does it do if a man heaps endearments on you, vows
that he is your friend, that he believes in you, is full of zeal for you,
esteems and loves you, and lauds you to the skies, when he rushes to do
the same to the first rapscallion he meets? No, no, no heart with the
least self-respect cares for esteem so prostituted; he will hardly relish it,
even when openly expressed, when he finds that he shares it with the
whole universe. Preference must be based on esteem, and to esteem
every one is to esteem no one. Since you abandon yourself to the vices
of the times, zounds! you are not the man for me. I decline this over-
complaisant kindness, which uses no discrimination. I like to be
distinguished; and, to cut the matter short, the friend of all mankind is
no friend of mine.

PHILINTE.   But when we are of the world, we must conform to the
outward civilities which custom demands.

ALCESTE.   I deny it. We ought to punish pitilessly that shameful pre-
tence of friendly intercourse. I like a man to be a man, and to show on
all occasions the bottom of his heart in his discourse. Let that be the
thing to speak, and never let our feelings be hidden beneath vain
compliments.

PHILINTE.   There are many cases in which plain speaking would become ridiculous, and could hardly be tolerated. And, with all due
allowance for your unbending honesty, it is as well to conceal your
feelings sometimes. Would it be right or decent to tell thousands of
people what we think of them? And when we meet with some one
whom we hate or who displeases us, must we tell him so openly?

ALCESTE. Yes.

PHILINTE. What! Would you tell old Emilia that it ill becomes her to set up for a beauty at her age, and that the paint she uses disgusts everyone?

ALCESTE. Undoubtedly.

PHILINTE. Or Dorilas, that he is a bore, and that there is no one at court who is not sick of hearing him boast of his courage, and the lustre of his house?

ALCESTE. Decidedly so.

PHILINTE. You are jesting.

ALCESTE. I am not jesting at all; and I would not spare any one in that respect. It offends my eyes too much; and whether at court or in town, I behold nothing but what provokes my spleen. I become quite melancholy and deeply grieved to see men behave to each other as they do. Everywhere I find nothing but base flattery, injustice, self-interest, deceit, roguery. I cannot bear it any longer; I am furious; and my intention is to break with all mankind.

PHILINTE. This philosophical spleen is somewhat too savage. I cannot but laugh to see you in these gloomy fits, and fancy that I perceive in us two, brought up together, the two brothers described in *The School for Husbands,** who . . .

ALCESTE. Good Heavens! drop your insipid comparisons.

PHILINTE. Nay, seriously, leave off these vagaries. The world will not alter for all your meddling. And as plain speaking has such charms for you, I shall tell you frankly that this complaint of yours is as good as a play, wherever you go, and that all those invectives against the manners of the age, make you a laughing stock to many people.

ALCESTE. So much the better, zounds! so much the better. That is just what I want. It is a very good sign, and I rejoice at it. All men are so odious to me, that I should be sorry to appear rational in their eyes.

PHILINTE. But do you wish harm to all mankind?

ALCESTE. Yes, I have conceived a terrible hatred for them.

PHILINTE. Shall all poor mortals, without exception, be included in this aversion? There are some, even in the age in which we live . . .

ALCESTE. No, they are all alike; and I hate all men: some, because they

* Molière's play *L'École des maris*, first performed in 1661.

are wicked and mischievous; others because they lend themselves to the wicked, and have not that healthy contempt with which vice ought to inspire all virtuous minds. You can see how unjustly and excessively complacent people are to that bare-faced scoundrel with whom I am at law. You may plainly perceive the traitor through his mask; he is well known everywhere in his true colors; his rolling eyes and his honeyed tones impose only on those who do not know him. People are aware that this low-bred fellow, who deserves to be pilloried, has, by the dirtiest jobs, made his way in the world; and that the splendid position he has acquired makes merit repine and virtue blush. Yet whatever dishonorable epithets may be launched against him everywhere, nobody defends his wretched honor. Call him a rogue, an infamous wretch, a confounded scoundrel if you like, all the world will say "yea," and no one contradicts you. But for all that, his bowing and scraping are welcome everywhere; he is received, smiled upon, and wriggles himself into all kinds of society; and, if any appointment is to be secured by intriguing, he will carry the day over a man of the greatest worth. Zounds! these are mortal stabs to me, to see vice parleyed with; and sometimes I feel suddenly inclined to fly into a wilderness far from the approach of men.

PHILINTE.   Great Heaven! let us torment ourselves a little less about the vices of our age, and be a little more lenient to human nature. Let us not scrutinize it with the utmost severity, but look with some indulgence at its failings. In society, we need virtue to be more pliable. If we are too wise, we may be equally to blame. Good sense avoids all extremes, and requires us to be soberly rational. This unbending and virtuous stiffness of ancient times shocks too much the ordinary customs of our own; it requires too great perfection from us mortals; we must yield to the times without being too stubborn; it is the height of folly to busy ourselves in correcting the world. I, as well as yourself, notice a hundred things every day which might be better managed, differently enacted; but whatever I may discover at any moment, people do not see me in a rage like you. I take men quietly just as they are; I accustom my mind to bear with what they do; and I believe that at court, as well as in the city, my phlegm is as philosophical as your bile.

ALCESTE.   But this phlegm, good sir, you who reason so well, could it not be disturbed by anything? And if perchance a friend should betray you; if he forms a subtle plot to get hold of what is yours; if people should try to spread evil reports about you, would you tamely submit to all this without flying into a rage?

PHILINTE.   Ay, I look upon all these faults of which you complain as vices inseparably connected with human nature; in short, my mind is no more shocked at seeing a man a rogue, unjust, or selfish, than at seeing vultures eager for prey, mischievous apes, or fury-lashed wolves.

ALCESTE.   What! I should see myself deceived, torn to pieces, robbed, without being . . . Zounds! I shall say no more about it; all this reasoning is beside the point!

PHILINTE.   Upon my word, you would do well to keep silence. Rail a little less at your opponents, and attend a little more to your suit.

ALCESTE.   That I shall not do; that is settled long ago.

PHILINTE.   But whom then do you expect to solicit for you?

ALCESTE.   Whom? Reason, my just right, equity.

PHILINTE.   Shall you not pay a visit to any of the judges?

ALCESTE.   No. Is my cause unjust or dubious?

PHILINTE.   I am agreed on that; but you know what harm intrigues do, and . . .

ALCESTE.   No. I am resolved not to stir a step. I am either right or wrong.

PHILINTE.   Do not trust to that.

ALCESTE.   I shall not budge an inch.

PHILINTE.   Your opponent is powerful, and by his underhand work, may induce . . .

ALCESTE.   It does not matter.

PHILINTE.   You will make a mistake.

ALCESTE.   Be it so. I wish to see the end of it.

PHILINTE.   But . . .

ALCESTE.   I shall have the satisfaction of losing my suit.

PHILINTE.   But after all . . .

ALCESTE.   I shall see by this trial whether men have sufficient impudence, are wicked, villainous, and perverse enough to do me this injustice in the face of the whole world.

PHILINTE.   What a strange fellow!

ALCESTE.   I could wish, were it to cost me ever so much, that, for the fun of the thing, I lost my case.

PHILINTE.   But people will really laugh at you, Alceste, if they hear you go on in this fashion.

ALCESTE.   So much the worse for those who will.

PHILINTE.   But this rectitude, which you exact so carefully in every case, this absolute integrity in which you intrench yourself, do you perceive it in the lady you love? As for me, I am astonished that, appearing to be at war with the whole human race, you yet, notwithstanding everything that can render it odious to you, have found aught to charm your eyes. And what surprises me still more, is the strange choice your heart has made. The sincere Éliante has a liking for you, the prude Arsinoé looks with favor upon you, yet your heart does not respond to their passion; whilst you wear the chains of Célimène, who sports with you, and whose coquettish humor and malicious wit seem to accord so well with the manner of the times. How comes it that, hating these things as mortally as you do, you endure so much of them in that lady? Are they no longer faults in so sweet a charmer? Do not you perceive them, or if you do, do you excuse them?

ALCESTE.   Not so. The love I feel for this young widow does not make me blind to her faults, and, notwithstanding the great passion with which she has inspired me, I am the first to see, as well as to condemn, them. But for all this, do what I will, I confess my weakness, she has the art of pleasing me. In vain I see her faults; I may even blame them; in spite of all, she makes me love her. Her charms conquer everything, and, no doubt, my sincere love will purify her heart from the vices of our times.

PHILINTE.   If you accomplish this, it will be no small task. Do you believe yourself beloved by her?

ALCESTE.   Yes, certainly! I should not love her at all, did I not think so.

PHILINTE.   But if her love for you is so apparent, how comes it that your rivals cause you so much uneasiness?

ALCESTE.   It is because a heart, deeply smitten, claims all to itself; I come here only with the intention of telling her what, on this subject, my feelings dictate.

PHILINTE.   Had I but to choose, her cousin Éliante would have all my love. Her heart, which values yours, is stable and sincere; and this more compatible choice would have suited you better.

ALCESTE.   It is true; my good sense tells me so every day; but good sense does not always rule love.

PHILINTE.   Well, I fear much for your affections; and the hope which you cherish may perhaps . . .

SCENE II.

ORONTE, ALCESTE, PHILINTE.

ORONTE.   [*To* ALCESTE] I have been informed yonder, that Éliante and
Célimène have gone out to make some purchases. But as I heard that
you were here, I came to tell you, most sincerely, that I have conceived
the greatest regard for you, and that, for a long time, this regard has
inspired me with the most ardent wish to be reckoned among your
friends. Yes; I like to do homage to merit; and I am most anxious that a
bond of friendship should unite us. I suppose that a zealous friend, and
of my standing, is not altogether to be rejected. [*All this time* ALCESTE
has been musing, and seems not to be aware that ORONTE *is addressing
him. He looks up only when* ORONTE *says to him*]—It is to you, if you
please, that this speech is addressed.

ALCESTE.   To me, sir?

ORONTE.   To you. Is it in any way offensive to you?

ALCESTE.   Not in the least. But my surprise is very great; and I did not
expect that honor.

ORONTE.   The regard in which I hold you ought not to astonish you,
and you claim it from the whole world.

ALCESTE.   Sir . . .

ORONTE.   Our whole kingdom contains nothing above the dazzling
merit which people discover in you.

ALCESTE.   Sir . . .

ORONTE.   Yes; for my part, I prefer you to the most important
in it.

ALCESTE.   Sir . . .

ORONTE.   May Heaven strike me dead, if I lie! And, to convince you,
on this very spot, of my feelings, allow me, sir, to embrace you with all
my heart, and to solicit a place in your friendship. Your hand, if you
please. Will you promise me your friendship?

ALCESTE.   Sir . . .

ORONTE.   What! you refuse me?

ALCESTE.   Sir, you do me too much honor; but friendship is a sacred
thing, and to lavish it on every occasion is surely to profane it.
Judgment and choice should preside at such a compact; we ought to
know more of each other before engaging ourselves; and it may happen

that our dispositions are such that we may both of us repent of our bargain.

ORONTE.   Upon my word! that is wisely said; and I esteem you all the more for it. Let us therefore leave it to time to form such a pleasing bond; but, meanwhile, I am entirely at your disposal. If you have any business at court, every one knows how well I stand with the King; I have his private ear; and, upon my word, he treats me in everything with the utmost intimacy. In short, I am yours in every emergency; and, as you are a man of brilliant parts, and to inaugurate our charming amity, I come to read you a sonnet which I made a little while ago, and to find out whether it be good enough for publicity.

ALCESTE.   I am not fit, sir, to decide such a matter. You will therefore excuse me.

ORONTE.   Why so?

ALCESTE.   I have the failing of being a little more sincere in those things than is necessary.

ORONTE.   The very thing I ask; and I should have reason to complain, if, in laying myself open to you that you might give me your frank opinion, you should deceive me, and disguise anything from me.

ALCESTE.   If that be the case, sir, I am perfectly willing.

ORONTE.   *Sonnet* . . . It is a sonnet . . . *Hope* . . . It is to a lady who flattered my passion with some hope. *Hope* . . . They are not long, pompous verses, but mild, tender and melting little lines. [*At every one of these interruptions he looks at* ALCESTE]

ALCESTE.   We shall see.

ORONTE.   Hope . . . I do not know whether the style will strike you as sufficiently clear and easy, and whether you will approve of my choice of words.

ALCESTE.   We shall soon see, sir.

ORONTE.   Besides, you must know that I was only a quarter of an hour in composing it.

ALCESTE.   Let us hear, sir; the time signifies nothing.

ORONTE. [*Reads*]

> *Hope, it is true, oft gives relief,*
> *Rocks for a while our tedious pain,*
> *But what a poor advantage, Phillis,*
> *When nought remains, and all is gone!*

PHILINTE.   I am already charmed with this little bit.

ALCESTE.   [*Softly to* PHILINTE] What! do you mean to tell me that you like this stuff?
ORONTE.

>   *You once showed some complaisance,*
>   *But less would have sufficed,*
>   *You should not take that trouble*
>   *To give me nought but hope.*

PHILINTE.   In what pretty terms these thoughts are put!
ALCESTE.   How now! you vile flatterer, you praise this rubbish!
ORONTE.

>   *If I must wait eternally,*
>   *My passion, driven to extremes,*
>   *Will fly to death.*
>   *Your tender cares cannot prevent this,*
>   *Fair Phillis, aye we're in despair,*
>   *When we must hope for ever.*

PHILINTE.   The conclusion is pretty, amorous, admirable.
ALCESTE.   [*Softly, and aside to* PHILINTE] A plague on the conclusion! I wish you had concluded to break your nose, you poisoner to the devil!
PHILINTE.   I never heard verses more skilfully turned.
ALCESTE.   [*Softly, and aside*] Zounds! . . .
ORONTE.   [*To* PHILINTE] You flatter me, and you are under the impression perhaps . . .
PHILINTE.   No, I am not flattering at all.
ALCESTE.   [*Softly, and aside*] What else are you doing, you wretch?
ORONTE.   [*To* ALCESTE] But for you, you know our agreement. Speak to me, I pray, in all sincerity.
ALCESTE.   These matters, sir, are always more or less delicate, and every one is fond of being praised for his wit. But I was saying one day to a certain person, who shall be nameless, when he showed me some of his verses, that a gentleman ought at all times to exercise a great control over that itch for writing which sometimes attacks us, and should keep a tight rein over the strong propensity which one has to display such amusements; and that, in the frequent anxiety to show their productions, people are frequently exposed to act a very foolish part.
ORONTE.   Do you wish to convey to me by this that I am wrong in desiring . . .

ALCESTE. I do not say that exactly. But I told him that writing without warmth becomes a bore; that there needs no other weakness to disgrace a man; that, even if people, on the other hand, had a hundred good qualities, we view them from their worst sides.

ORONTE. Do you find anything to object to in my sonnet?

ALCESTE. I do not say that. But, to keep him from writing, I set before his eyes how, in our days, that desire had spoiled a great many very worthy people.

ORONTE. Do I write badly? Am I like them in any way?

ALCESTE. I do not say that. But, in short, I said to him: What pressing need is there for you to rhyme, and what the deuce drives you into print? If we can pardon the sending into the world of a badly-written book, it will only be in those unfortunate men who write for their livelihood. Believe me, resist your temptations, keep these effusions from the public, and do not, how much soever you may be asked, forfeit the reputation which you enjoy at court of being a man of sense and a gentleman, to take, from the hands of a greedy printer, that of a ridiculous and wretched author. That is what I tried to make him understand.

ORONTE. This is all well and good, and I seem to understand you. But I should like to know what there is in my sonnet to . . .

ALCESTE. Candidly, you had better put it in your closet. You have been following bad models, and your expressions are not at all natural. Pray what is—*Rocks for a while our tedious pain?* And what, *When nought remains, and all is gone?* What, *You should not take that trouble to give me nought but hope?* And what, *Phillis, aye we're in despair when we must hope for ever?* This figurative style, that people are so vain of, is beside all good taste and truth; it is only a play upon words, sheer affectation, and it is not thus that nature speaks. The wretched taste of the age is what I dislike in this. Our forefathers, unpolished as they were, had a much better one; and I value all that is admired now-a-days far less than an old song which I am going to repeat to you:

> Had our great monarch granted me
> His Paris large and fair;
> And I straightway must quit for aye
> The love of my true dear;
> Then would I say, King Hal, I pray,
> Take back your Paris fair,
> I love much mo my dear, I trow,
> I love ntuch mo my dear.

This versification is not rich, and the style is antiquated; but do you not see that it is far better than all those trumpery trifles against which good sense revolts, and that in this, passion speaks from the heart?

> Had our great monarch granted me
> His Paris large and fair;
> And I straightway must quit for aye
> The love of my true dear;
> Then would I say, King Hal, I pray,
> Take back your Paris fair,
> I love much mo my dear, I trow,
> I love much mo my dear.

This is what a really loving heart would say. [To PHILINTE, *who is laughing*] Yes, master wag, in spite of all your wit, I care more for this than for all the florid pomp and the tinsel which everybody is admiring now-a-days.

ORONTE.   And I, I maintain that my verses are very good.

ALCESTE.   Doubtless you have your reasons for thinking them so; but you will allow me to have mine, which, with your permission, will remain independent.

ORONTE.   It is enough for me that others prize them.

ALCESTE.   That is because they know how to dissemble, which I do not.

ORONTE.   Do you really believe that you have such a great share of wit?

ALCESTE.   If I praised your verses, I should have more.

ORONTE.   I shall do very well without your approbation.

ALCESTE.   You will have to do without it, if it be all the same.

ORONTE.   I should like much to see you compose some on the same subject, just to have a sample of your style.

ALCESTE.   I might, perchance, make some as bad; but I should take good care not to show them to any one.

ORONTE.   You are mighty positive; and this great sufficiency . . .

ALCESTE.   Pray, seek some one else to flatter you, and not me.

ORONTE.   But, my little sir, drop this haughty tone.

ALCESTE.   In truth, my big sir, I shall do as I like.

PHILINTE.   [*Coming between them*] Stop, gentlemen! that is carrying the matter too far. Cease, I pray.

ORONTE.   Ah! I am wrong, I confess; and I leave the field to you. I am your servant, sir, most heartily.

ALCESTE.   And I, sir, am your most humble servant.

SCENE III.

PHILINTE, ALCESTE.

PHILINTE.   Well! you see. By being too sincere, you have got a nice
   affair on your hands; I saw that Oronte, in order to be flattered . . .
ALCESTE.   Do not talk to me.
PHILINTE.   But . . .
ALCESTE.   No more society for me.
PHILINTE.   Is it too much . . .
ALCESTE.   Leave me alone.
PHILINTE.   If I . . .
ALCESTE.   Not another word.
PHILINTE.   But what . . .
ALCESTE.   I will hear no more.
PHILINTE.   But . . .
ALCESTE.   Again?
PHILINTE.   People insult . . .
ALCESTE.   Ah! Zounds! this is too much. Do not dog my steps.
PHILINTE.   You are making fun of me; I shall not leave you.

ACT II.

SCENE I.

ALCESTE, CÉLIMÈNE.

ALCESTE. Will you have me speak candidly to you, Madam? Well, then, I am very much dissatisfied with your behavior. I am very angry when I think of it; and I perceive that we shall have to break with each other. Yes; I should only deceive you were I to speak otherwise. Sooner or later a rupture is unavoidable; and if I were to promise the contrary a thousand times, I should not be able to bear this any longer.

CÉLIMÈNE. Oh, I see! it is to quarrel with me, that you wished to conduct me home?

ALCESTE. I do not quarrel. But your disposition, Madam, is too ready to give any first comer an entrance into your heart. Too many admirers beset you; and my temper cannot put up with that.

CÉLIMÈNE. Am I to blame for having too many admirers? Can I prevent people from thinking me amiable? and am I to take a stick to drive them away, when they endeavor by tender means to visit me?

ALCESTE. No, Madam, there is no need for a stick, but only a heart less yielding and less melting at their love-tales. I am aware that your good looks accompany you, go where you will; but your reception retains those whom your eyes attract; and that gentleness, accorded to those who surrender their arms, finishes on their hearts the sway which your charms began. The too agreeable expectation which you offer them increases their assiduities towards you; and your complacency, a little less extended, would drive away the great crowd of so many admirers. But tell me, at least, Madam, by what good fortune Clitandre has the happiness of pleasing you so mightily? Upon what basis of merit and sublime virtue do you ground the honor of your regard for him? Is it by the long nail on his little finger that he has acquired the esteem which

13

you display for him? Are you, like all the rest of the fashionable world, fascinated by the dazzling merit of his fair wig? Do his great rolls make you love him? Do his many ribbons charm you? Is it by the attraction of his great German breeches that he has conquered your heart, whilst at the same time he pretended to be your slave? Or have his manner of smiling, and his falsetto voice, found out the secret of moving your feelings?

CÉLIMÈNE.   How unjustly you take umbrage at him! Do not you know why I countenance him; and that he has promised to interest all his friends in my lawsuit?

ALCESTE.   Lose your lawsuit, Madam, with patience, and do not countenance a rival whom I detest.

CÉLIMÈNE.   But you are getting jealous of the whole world.

ALCESTE.   It is because the whole world is so kindly received by you.

CÉLIMÈNE.   That is the very thing to calm your frightened mind, because my good-will is diffused over all: you would have more reason to be offended if you saw me entirely occupied with one.

ALCESTE.   But as for me, whom you accuse of too much jealousy, what have I more than any of them, Madam, pray?

CÉLIMÈNE.   The happiness of knowing that you are beloved.

ALCESTE.   And what grounds has my lovesick heart for believing it?

CÉLIMÈNE.   I think that, as I have taken the trouble to tell you so, such an avowal ought to satisfy you.

ALCESTE.   But who will assure me that you may not, at the same time, say as much to everybody else perhaps?

CÉLIMÈNE.   Certainly, for a lover, this is a pretty amorous speech, and you make me out a very nice lady. Well! to remove such a suspicion, I retract this moment everything I have said; and no one but yourself shall for the future impose upon you. Will that satisfy you?

ALCESTE.   Zounds! why do I love you so! Ah! if ever I get heart-whole out of your hands, I shall bless Heaven for this rare good fortune. I make no secret of it; I do all that is possible to tear this unfortunate attachment from my heart; but hitherto my greatest efforts have been of no avail; and it is for my sins that I love you thus.

CÉLIMÈNE.   It is very true that your affection for me is unequaled.

ALCESTE.   As for that, I can challenge the whole world. My love for you cannot be conceived; and never, Madam, has any man loved as I do.

CÉLIMÈNE.   Your method, however, is entirely new, for you love people only to quarrel with them; it is in peevish expression alone that your feelings vent themselves; no one ever saw such a grumbling swain.

ALCESTE.   But it lies with you alone to dissipate this ill-humor. For mercy's sake let us make an end of all these bickerings; deal openly with each other, and try to put a stop . . .

SCENE II.

CÉLIMÈNE, ALCESTE, BASQUE.

CÉLIMÈNE.   What is the matter?
BASQUE.   Acaste is below.
CÉLIMÈNE.   Very well! bid him come up.

SCENE III.

CÉLIMÈNE, ALCESTE.

ALCESTE.   What! can one never have a little private conversation with you? You are always ready to receive company; and you cannot, for a single instant, make up your mind to be "not at home."
CÉLIMÈNE.   Do you wish me to quarrel with Acaste?
ALCESTE.   You have such regard for people, which I by no means like.
CÉLIMÈNE.   He is a man never to forgive me, if he knew that his presence could annoy me.
ALCESTE.   And what is that to you, to inconvenience yourself so . . .
CÉLIMÈNE.   But, good Heaven! the amity of such as he is of importance; they are a kind of people who, I do not know how, have acquired the right to be heard at court. They take their part in every conversation; they can do you no good, but they may do you harm; and, whatever support one may find elsewhere, it will never do to be on bad terms with these very noisy gentry.
ALCESTE.   In short, whatever people may say or do, you always find reasons to bear with every one; and your very careful judgment . . .

SCENE IV.

ALCESTE, CÉLIMÈNE, BASQUE.

BASQUE. Clitandre is here, too, Madam.
ALCESTE. Exactly so. [*Wishes to go*]
CÉLIMÈNE. Where are you running to?
ALCESTE. I am going.
CÉLIMÈNE. Stay.
ALCESTE. For what?
CÉLIMÈNE. Stay.
ALCESTE. I cannot.
CÉLIMÈNE. I wish it.
ALCESTE. I will not. These conversations only weary me; and it is too bad of you to wish me to endure them.
CÉLIMÈNE. I wish it, I wish it.
ALCESTE. No, it is impossible.
CÉLIMÈNE. Very well, then; go, begone; you can do as you like.

SCENE V.

ÉLIANTE, PHILINTE, ACASTE, CLITANDRE, ALCESTE, CÉLIMÈNE, BASQUE.

ÉLIANTE. [*To* CÉLIMÈNE] Here are the two marquises coming up with us. Has anyone told you?
CÉLIMÈNE. Yes. [*To* BASQUE] Place chairs for everyone. [BASQUE *places chairs, and goes out*] [*To* ALCESTE] You are not gone?
ALCESTE. No; but I am determined, Madam, to have you make up your mind either for them or for me.
CÉLIMÈNE. Hold your tongue.
ALCESTE. This very day you shall explain yourself.
CÉLIMÈNE. You are losing your senses.
ALCESTE. Not at all. You shall declare yourself.
CÉLIMÈNE. Indeed!
ALCESTE. You must take your stand.
CÉLIMÈNE. You are jesting, I believe.

ALCESTE.   Not so. But you must choose. I have been too patient.

CLITANDRE.   Egad! I have just come from the Louvre, where Cléonte, at the levee, made himself very ridiculous. Has he not some friend who could charitably enlighten him upon his manners?

CÉLIMÈNE.   Truth to say, he compromises himself very much in society; everywhere he carries himself with an air that is noticed at first sight, and when after a short absence you meet him again, he is still more absurd than ever.

ACASTE.   Egad! Talk of absurd people, just now, one of the most tedious ones was annoying me. That reasoner, Damon, kept me, if you please, for a full hour in the broiling sun, away from my sedan-chair.

CÉLIMÈNE.   He is a strange talker, and one who always finds the means of telling you nothing with a great flow of words. There is no sense at all in his tittle-tattle, and all that we hear is but noise.

ÉLIANTE.   [To PHILINTE] This beginning is not bad; and the conversation takes a sufficiently agreeable turn against our neighbors.

CLITANDRE.   Timante, too, Madam, is another original.

CÉLIMÈNE.   He is a complete mystery from top to toe, who throws upon you, in passing, a bewildered glance, and who, without having anything to do, is always busy. Whatever he utters is accompanied with grimaces; he quite oppresses people by his ceremonies. To interrupt a conversation, he has always a secret to whisper to you, and that secret turns out to be nothing. Of the merest molehill he makes a mountain, and whispers everything in your ear, even to a "good-day."

ACASTE.   And Geralde, Madam?

CÉLIMÈNE.   That tiresome story-teller! He never comes down from his nobleman's pedestal; he continually mixes with the best society, and never quotes any one of minor rank than a Duke, Prince, or Princess. Rank is his hobby, and his conversation is of nothing but horses, carriages, and dogs. He thee's and thou's persons of the highest standing, and the word Sir is quite obsolete with him.

CLITANDRE.   It is said that he is on the best of terms with Bélise.

CÉLIMÈNE.   Poor silly woman, and the dreariest company! When she comes to visit me, I suffer from martyrdom; one has to rack one's brain perpetually to find out what to say to her; and the impossibility of her expressing her thoughts allows the conversation to drop every minute. In vain you try to overcome her stupid silence by the assistance of the most commonplace topic; even the fine weather, the rain, the heat and the cold are subjects, which, with her, are soon exhausted. Yet for all that, her calls, unbearable enough, are prolonged to an insufferable length; and you may consult the clock, or yawn twenty times, but she stirs no more than a log of wood.

ACASTE.   What think you of Adraste?

CÉLIMÈNE.   Oh! What excessive pride! He is a man positively puffed out with conceit. His self-importance is never satisfied with the court, against which he inveighs daily; and whenever an office, a place, or a living is bestowed on another, he is sure to think himself unjustly treated.

CLITANDRE.   But young Cléon, whom the most respectable people go to see, what say you of him?

CÉLIMÈNE.   That it is to his cook he owes his distinction, and to his table that people pay visits.

ÉLIANTE.   He takes pains to provide the most dainty dishes.

CÉLIMÈNE.   True; but I should be very glad if he would not dish up himself. His foolish person is a very bad dish, which, to my thinking, spoils every entertainment which he gives.

PHILINTE.   His uncle Damis is very much esteemed; what say you to him, Madam?

CÉLIMÈNE.   He is one of my friends.

PHILINTE.   I think him a perfect gentleman, and sensible enough.

CÉLIMÈNE.   True; but he pretends to too much wit, which annoys me. He is always upon stilts, and, in all his conversations, one sees him laboring to say smart things. Since he took it into his head to be clever, he is so difficult to please that nothing suits his taste. He must needs find mistakes in everything that one writes, and thinks that to bestow praise does not become a wit, that to find fault shows learning, that only fools admire and laugh, and that, by not approving of anything in the works of our time, he is superior to all other people. Even in conversations he finds something to cavil at, the subjects are too trivial for his condescension; and, with arms crossed on his breast, he looks down from the height of his intellect with pity on what everyone says.

ACASTE.   Drat it! his very picture.

CLITANDRE.   [To CÉLIMÈNE] You have an admirable knack of portraying people to the life.

ALCESTE.   Capital, go on, my fine courtly friends. You spare no one, and everyone will have his turn. Nevertheless, let but any one of those persons appear, and we shall see you rush to meet him, offer him your hand, and, with a flattering kiss, give weight to your protestations of being his servant.

CLITANDRE.   Why this to us? If what is said offends you, the reproach must be addressed to this lady.

ALCESTE.   No, gadzooks! it concerns you; for your assenting smiles draw from her wit all these slanderous remarks. Her satirical vein is incessantly recruited by the culpable incense of your flattery; and her mind would find fewer charms in raillery, if she discovered that no one applauded her. Thus it is that to flatterers we ought everywhere to impute the vices which are sown among mankind.

PHILINTE.   But why do you take so great an interest in those people, for you would condemn the very things that are blamed in them?

CÉLIMÈNE.   And is not this gentleman bound to contradict? Would you have him subscribe to the general opinion; and must he not everywhere display the spirit of contradiction with which Heaven has endowed him? Other people's sentiments can never please him. He always supports a contrary idea, and he would think himself too much of the common herd, were he observed to be of any one's opinion but his own. The honor of gainsaying has so many charms for him, that he very often takes up the cudgels against himself; he combats his own sentiments as soon as he hears them from other folks' lips.

ALCESTE.   In short, Madam, the laughers are on your side; and you may launch your satire against me.

PHILINTE.   But it is very true, too, that you always take up arms against everything that is said; and that your avowed spleen cannot bear people to be praised or blamed.

ALCESTE.   'Sdeath! spleen against mankind is always seasonable, because they are never in the right, and I see that, in all their dealings, they either praise impertinently, or censure rashly.

CÉLIMÈNE.   But . . .

ALCESTE.   No, Madam, no, though I were to die for it, you have pastimes which I cannot tolerate; and people are very wrong to nourish in your heart this great attachment to the very faults which they blame in you.

CLITANDRE.   As for myself, I do not know; but I openly acknowledge that hitherto I have thought this lady faultless.

ACASTE.   I see that she is endowed with charms and attractions; but the faults which she has have not struck me.

ALCESTE.   So much the more have they struck me; and far from appearing blind, she knows that I take care to reproach her with them. The more we love any one, the less we ought to flatter her. True love shows itself by overlooking nothing; and, were I a lady, I would banish all those mean-spirited lovers who submit to all my sentiments, and whose mild complacencies every moment offer up incense to my vagaries.

CÉLIMÈNE.   In short, if hearts were ruled by you we ought, to love well, to relinquish all tenderness, and make it the highest aim of perfect attachment to rail heartily at the persons we love.

ÉLIANTE.   Love, generally speaking, is little apt to put up with these decrees, and lovers are always observed to extol their choice. Their passion never sees aught to blame in it, and in the beloved all things become lovable. They think their faults perfections, and invent sweet terms to call them by. The pale one vies with the jessamine in fairness; another, dark enough to frighten people, becomes an adorable brunette; the lean one has a good shape and is lithe; the stout one has a portly and majestic bearing; the slattern, who has few charms, passes under the name of a careless beauty; the giantess seems a very goddess in their sight; the dwarf is an epitome of all the wonders of Heaven; the proud one has a soul worthy of a diadem; the artful brims with wit; the silly one is very good-natured; the chatterbox is good-tempered; and the silent one modest and reticent. Thus a passionate swain loves even the very faults of those of whom he is enamored.

ALCESTE.   And I maintain that . . .

CÉLIMÈNE.   Let us drop the subject, and take a turn or two in the gallery. What! are you going, gentlemen?

CLITANDRE *and* ACASTE.   No, no, Madam.

ALCESTE.   The fear of their departure troubles you very much. Go when you like, gentlemen; but I tell you beforehand that I shall not leave until you leave.

ACASTE.   Unless it inconveniences this lady, I have nothing to call me elsewhere the whole day.

CLITANDRE.   I, provided I am present when the King retires, I have no other matter to call me away.

CÉLIMÈNE.   [*To* ALCESTE] You only joke, I fancy.

ALCESTE.   Not at all. We shall soon see whether it is me of whom you wish to get rid.

SCENE VI.

ALCESTE, CÉLIMÈNE, ÉLIANTE, ACASTE, PHILINTE, CLITANDRE, BASQUE.

BASQUE. [To ALCESTE] There is a man downstairs, sir, who wishes to speak to you on business which cannot be postponed.
ALCESTE. Tell him that I have no such urgent business.
BASQUE. He wears a jacket with large plaited skirts embroidered with gold.
CÉLIMÈNE. [To ALCESTE] Go and see who it is, or else let him come in.

SCENE VII.

ALCESTE, CÉLIMÈNE, ÉLIANTE, ACASTE, PHILINTE, CLITANDRE, a Guard of the Maréchaussée.

ALCESTE. [Going to meet the Guard] What may be your pleasure? Come in, sir.
GUARD. I would have a few words privately with you, sir.
ALCESTE. You may speak aloud, sir, so as to let me know.
GUARD. The Marshals of France, whose commands I bear, hereby summon you to appear before them immediately, sir.
ALCESTE. Whom? Me, sir?
GUARD. Yourself.
ALCESTE. And for what?
PHILINTE. [To ALCESTE] It is this ridiculous affair between you and Oronte.
CÉLIMÈNE. [To PHILINTE] What do you mean?
PHILINTE. Oronte and he have been insulting each other just now about some trifling verses which he did not like; and the Marshals wish to nip the affair in the bud.
ALCESTE. Well, I shall never basely submit.
PHILINTE. But you must obey the summons: come, get ready.
ALCESTE. How will they settle this between us? Will the edict of these gentlemen oblige me to approve of the verses which are the cause of

our quarrel? I will not retract what I have said; I think them abominable.

PHILINTE.   But with a little milder tone . . .

ALCESTE.   I will not abate one jot; the verses are execrable.

PHILINTE.   You ought to show a more accommodating spirit. Come along.

ALCESTE.   I shall go, but nothing shall induce me to retract.

PHILINTE.   Go and show yourself.

ALCESTE.   Unless an express order from the King himself commands me to approve of the verses which cause all this trouble, I shall ever maintain, egad, that they are bad, and that a fellow deserves hanging for making them. [*To* CLITANDRE *and* ACASTE, *who are laughing*] Hang it! gentlemen, I did not think I was so amusing.

CÉLIMÈNE.   Go quickly whither you are wanted.

ALCESTE.   I am going, Madam; but shall come back here to finish our discussion.

ACT III.

CLITANDRE, ACASTE.

CLITANDRE. My dear marquis, you appear mightily pleased with your-self; everything amuses you, and nothing discomposes you. But really and truly, think you, without flattering yourself, that you have good reasons for appearing so joyful?

ACASTE. Egad, I do not find, on looking at myself, any matter to be sorrowful about. I am wealthy, I am young, and am descended from a family which, with some appearance of truth, may be called noble; and I think that, by the rank which my lineage confers upon me, there are very few offices to which I might not aspire. As for courage, which we ought especially to value, it is well known—this without vanity—that I do not lack it; and people have seen me carry on an affair of honor in a manner sufficiently vigorous and brisk. As for wit, I have some, no doubt; and as for good taste, to judge and reason upon everything without study; at "first nights," of which I am very fond, to take my place as a critic upon the stage, to give my opinion as a judge, to applaud, and point out the best passages by repeated bravoes, I am sufficiently adroit; I carry myself well, and am good-looking, have particularly fine teeth, and a good figure. I believe, without flattering myself, that, as for dressing in good taste, very few will dispute the palm with me. I find myself treated with every possible consideration, very much beloved by the fair sex; and I stand very well with the King. With all that, I think, dear marquis, that one might be satisfied with oneself anywhere.

CLITANDRE. True. But, finding so many easy conquests elsewhere, why come you here to utter fruitless sighs?

ACASTE. I? Zounds! I have neither the wish nor the disposition to put

23

up with the indifference of any woman. I leave it to awkward and ordinary people to burn constantly for cruel fair maidens, to languish at their feet, and to bear with their severities, to invoke the aid of sighs and tears, and to endeavor, by long and persistent assiduities, to obtain what is denied to their little merit. But men of my stamp, marquis, are not made to love on trust, and be at all the expenses themselves. Be the merit of the fair ever so great, I think, thank Heaven, that we have our value as well as they; that it is not reasonable to enthrall a heart like mine without its costing them anything; and that, to weigh everything in a just scale, the advances should be, at least, reciprocal.

CLITANDRE. Then you think that you are right enough here, marquis?

ACASTE. I have some reason, marquis, to think so.

CLITANDRE. Believe me, divest yourself of this great mistake: you flatter yourself, dear friend, and are altogether self-deceived.

ACASTE. It is true. I flatter myself, and am, in fact, altogether self-deceived.

CLITANDRE. But what causes you to judge your happiness to be complete?

ACASTE. I flatter myself.

CLITANDRE. Upon what do you ground your belief?

ACASTE. I am altogether self-deceived.

CLITANDRE. Have you any sure proofs?

ACASTE. I am mistaken, I tell you.

CLITANDRE. Has Célimène made you any secret avowal of her inclinations?

ACASTE. No, I am very badly treated by her.

CLITANDRE. Answer me, I pray.

ACASTE. I meet with nothing but rebuffs.

CLITANDRE. A truce to your raillery; and tell me what hope she has held out to you.

ACASTE. I am the rejected, and you are the lucky one. She has a great aversion to me, and one of these days I shall have to hang myself.

CLITANDRE. Nonsense. Shall we two, marquis, to adjust our love affairs, make a compact together? Whenever one of us shall be able to show a certain proof of having the greater share in Célimène's heart, the other shall leave the field free to the supposed conqueror, and by that means rid him of an obstinate rival.

ACASTE. Egad! you please me with these words, and I agree to that from the bottom of my heart. But, hush.

SCENE II.

CÉLIMÈNE, ACASTE, CLITANDRE.

CÉLIMÈNE.   What! here still?
CLITANDRE.   Love, Madam, detains us.
CÉLIMÈNE.   I hear a carriage below. Do you know whose it is?
CLITANDRE.   No.

SCENE III.

CÉLIMÈNE, ACASTE, CLITANDRE, BASQUE.

BASQUE.   Arsinoé, Madam, is coming up to see you.
CÉLIMÈNE.   What does the woman want with me?
BASQUE.   Éliante is downstairs talking to her.
CÉLIMÈNE.   What is she thinking about, and what brings her here?
ACASTE.   She has everywhere the reputation of being a consummate prude, and her fervent zeal . . .
CÉLIMÈNE.   Psha, downright humbug. In her inmost soul she is as worldly as any; and her every nerve is strained to hook some one, without being successful, however. She can only look with envious eyes on the accepted lovers of others; and in her wretched condition, forsaken by all, she is for ever railing against the blindness of the age. She endeavors to hide the dreadful isolation of her home under a false cloak of prudishness; and to save the credit of her feeble charms, she brands as criminal the power which they lack. Yet a swain would not come at all amiss to the lady; and she has even a tender hankering after Alceste. Every attention that he pays me, she looks upon as a theft committed by me, and as an insult to her attractions; and her jealous spite, which she can hardly hide, breaks out against me at every opportunity, and in an underhand manner. In short, I never saw anything, to my fancy, so stupid. She is impertinent to the last degree . . .

SCENE IV.

ARSINOÉ, CÉLIMÈNE, CLITANDRE, ACASTE.

CÉLIMÈNE. Ah! what happy chance brings you here, Madam? I was really getting uneasy about you.
ARSINOÉ. I have come to give you some advice as a matter of duty.
CÉLIMÈNE. How very glad I am to see you!

[*Exeunt* CLITANDRE *and* ACASTE, *laughing*]

SCENE V.

ARSINOÉ, CÉLIMÈNE.

ARSINOÉ. They could not have left at a more convenient opportunity.
CÉLIMÈNE. Shall we sit down?
ARSINOÉ. It is not necessary. Friendship, Madam, must especially show itself in matters which may be of consequence to us; and as there are none of greater importance than honor and decorum, I come to prove to you, by an advice which closely touches your reputation, the friendship which I feel for you. Yesterday I was with some people of rare virtue, where the conversation turned upon you; and there, your conduct, which is causing some stir, was unfortunately, Madam, far from being commended. That crowd of people, whose visits you permit, your gallantry and the noise it makes, were criticized rather more freely and more severely than I could have wished. You can easily imagine whose part I took. I did all I could to defend you. I exonerated you, and vouched for the purity of your heart, and the honesty of your intentions. But you know there are things in life which one cannot well defend, although one may have the greatest wish to do so; and I was at last obliged to confess that the way in which you lived did you some harm; that, in the eyes of the world, it had a doubtful look; that there was no story so ill-natured as not to be everywhere told about it; and that, if you liked, your behavior might give less cause for censure. Not that I believe that decency is in any way outraged. Heaven forbid that I should harbor such a thought! But the

world is so ready to give credit to the faintest shadow of a crime, and it is not enough to live blameless one's self. Madam, I believe you to be too sensible not to take in good part this useful counsel, and not to ascribe it only to the inner promptings of an affection that feels an interest in your welfare.

CÉLIMÈNE.   Madam, I have a great many thanks to return you. Such counsel lays me under an obligation; and, far from taking it amiss, I intend this very moment to repay the favor, by giving you an advice which also touches your reputation closely; and as I see you prove yourself my friend by acquainting me with the stories that are current of me, I shall follow so nice an example, by informing you what is said of you. In a house the other day, where I paid a visit, I met some people of exemplary merit, who, while talking of the proper duties of a well spent life, turned the topic of the conversation upon you, Madam. There your prudishness and your too fervent zeal were not at all cited as a good example. This affectation of a grave demeanor, your eternal conversations on wisdom and honor, your mincings and mouthings at the slightest shadows of indecency, which an innocent though ambiguous word may convey, that lofty esteem in which you hold yourself, and those pitying glances which you cast upon all, your frequent lectures and your acrid censures on things which are pure and harmless; all this, if I may speak frankly to you, Madam, was blamed unanimously. What is the good, said they, of this modest mien and this prudent exterior, which is belied by all the rest? She says her prayers with the utmost exactness; but she beats her servants and pays them no wages. She displays great fervor in every place of devotion; but she paints and wishes to appear handsome. She covers the nudities in her pictures; but loves the reality. As for me, I undertook your defence against everyone, and positively assured them that it was nothing but scandal; but the general opinion went against me, as they came to the conclusion that you would do well to concern yourself less about the actions of others, and take a little more pains with your own; that one ought to look a long time at one's self before thinking of condemning other people; that when we wish to correct others, we ought to add the weight of a blameless life; and that even then, it would be better to leave it to those whom Heaven has ordained for the task. Madam, I also believe you to be too sensible not to take in good part this useful counsel, and not to ascribe it only to the inner promptings of an affection that feels an interest in your welfare.

ARSINOÉ. To whatever we may be exposed when we reprove, I did not expect this retort, Madam, and, by its very sting, I see how my sincere advice has hurt your feelings.

CÉLIMÈNE. On the contrary, Madam; and, if we were reasonable, these mutual counsels would become customary. If honestly made use of, they would to a great extent destroy the excellent opinion people have of themselves. It depends entirely on you whether we shall continue this trustworthy practice with equal zeal, and whether we shall take great care to tell each other, between ourselves, what we hear, you of me, I of you.

ARSINOÉ. Ah! Madam, I can hear nothing said of you. It is in me that people find so much to reprove.

CÉLIMÈNE. Madam, it is easy, I believe, to blame or praise everything; and everyone may be right, according to their age and taste. There is a time for gallantry, there is one also for prudishness. One may out of policy take to it, when youthful attractions have faded away. It sometimes serves to hide vexatious ravages of time. I do not say that I shall not follow your example, one of these days. Those things come with old age; but twenty, as everyone well knows, is not an age to play the prude.

ARSINOÉ. You certainly pride yourself upon a very small advantage, and you boast terribly of your age. Whatever difference there may be between your years and mine, there is no occasion to make such a tremendous fuss about it; and I am at a loss to know, Madam, why you should get so angry, and what makes you goad me in this manner.

CÉLIMÈNE. And I, Madam, am at an equal loss to know why one hears you inveigh so bitterly against me everywhere. Must I always suffer for your vexations? Can I help it, if people refuse to pay you any attentions? If men will fall in love with me, and will persist in offering me each day those attentions of which your heart would wish to see me deprived, I cannot alter it, and it is not my fault. I leave you the field free, and do not prevent you from having charms to attract people.

ARSINOÉ. Alas! and do you think that I would trouble myself about this crowd of lovers of which you are so vain, and that it is not very easy to judge at what price they may be attracted now-a-days? Do you wish to make it be believed, that, judging by what is going on, your merit alone attracts this crowd; that their affection for you is strictly honest, and that it is for nothing but your virtue that they all pay you their court? People are not blinded by those empty pretences; the world is not duped in that way; and I see many ladies who are capable of inspiring a tender feeling, yet who do not succeed in attracting a crowd of beaux; and from that fact we may draw our conclusion that those conquests are not altogether made without some great advances; that no one cares to sigh for us, for our handsome looks only; and that the attentions bestowed on us are generally dearly bought. Do not therefore pull yourself up with vain-glory about the trifling advantages of a poor victory; and moderate slightly the pride on your good looks, instead of looking down upon people on account of them. If I were at all envious about your conquests, I dare say that I might manage like other people; be under no restraint, and thus show plainly that one may have lovers, when one wishes for them.

CÉLIMÈNE.   Do have some then, Madam, and let us see you try it; endeavor to please by this extraordinary secret; and without . . .

ARSINOÉ.   Let us break off this conversation, Madam, it might excite too much both your temper and mine; and I would have already taken my leave, had I not been obliged to wait for my carriage.

CÉLIMÈNE.   Please stay as long as you like, and do not hurry yourself on that account, Madam. But instead of wearying you any longer with my presence, I am going to give you some more pleasant company. This gentleman, who comes very opportunely, will better supply my place in entertaining you.

SCENE VI.

ALCESTE, CÉLIMÈNE, ARSINOÉ.

CÉLIMÈNE.   Alceste, I have to write a few lines, which I cannot well delay. Please to stay with this lady; she will all the more easily excuse my rudeness.

SCENE VII.

ALCESTE, ARSINOÉ.

ARSINOÉ.   You see, I am left here to entertain you, until my coach comes round. She could have devised no more charming treat for me, than such a conversation. Indeed, people of exceptional merit attract the esteem and love of every one; and yours has undoubtedly some secret charm, which makes me feel interested in all your doings. I could wish that the court, with a real regard to your merits, would do more justice to your deserts. You have reason to complain; and it vexes me to see that day by day nothing is done for you.

ALCESTE.   For me, Madam? And by what right could I pretend to anything? What service have I rendered to the State? Pray, what have I done, so brilliant in itself, to complain of the court doing nothing for me?

ARSINOÉ.   Not everyone whom the State delights to honor, has rendered signal services; there must be an opportunity as well as the power; and the abilities which you allow us to perceive, ought . . .

ALCESTE.   For Heaven's sake, let us have no more of my abilities, I pray. What would you have the court to do? It would have enough to do, and have its hands full, to discover the merits of people.

ARSINOÉ.   Sterling merit discovers itself. A great deal is made of yours in certain places; and let me tell you that, not later than yesterday, you were highly spoken of in two distinguished circles, by people of very great standing.

ALCESTE.   As for that, Madam, everyone is praised now-a-days, and very little discrimination is shown in our times. Everything is equally endowed with great merit, so that it is no longer an honor to be lauded. Praises abound, they throw them at one's head, and even my valet is put in the gazette.

ARSINOÉ.   As for me, I could wish that, to bring yourself into greater notice, some place at court might tempt you. If you will only give me a hint that you seriously think about it, a great many engines might be set in motion to serve you; and I know some people whom I could employ for you, and who would manage the matter smoothly enough.

ALCESTE.   And what should I do when I got there, Madam? My disposition rather prompts me to keep away from it. Heaven, when ushering me into the world, did not give me a mind suited for the atmosphere of a court. I have not the qualifications necessary for success, nor for making my fortune there. To be open and candid is my chief talent; I possess not the art of deceiving people in conversation; and he who has not the gift of concealing his thoughts, ought not to stay long in those places. When not at court, one has not, doubtless, that standing, and the advantage of those honorable titles which it bestows now-a-days;

but, on the other hand, one has not the vexation of playing the silly fool. One has not to bear a thousand galling rebuffs; one is not, as it were, forced to praise the verses of Mister so-and-so, to laud Madam such and such, and to put up with the whims of some ingenious marquis.

ARSINOÉ.   Since you wish it, let us drop the subject of the court: but I cannot help grieving for your amours; and, to tell you my opinions candidly on that head, I could heartily wish your affections better bestowed. You certainly deserve a much happier fate, and she who has fascinated you is unworthy of you.

ALCESTE.   But in saying so, Madam, remember, I pray, that this lady is your friend.

ARSINOÉ.   True. But really my conscience revolts at the thought of suffering any longer the wrong that is done to you. The position in which I see you afflicts my very soul, and I caution you that your affections are betrayed.

ALCESTE.   This is certainly showing me a deal of good feeling, Madam, and such information is very welcome to a lover.

ARSINOÉ.   Yes, for all Célimène is my friend, I do not hesitate to call her unworthy of possessing the heart of a man of honor; and hers only pretends to respond to yours.

ALCESTE.   That is very possible, Madam, one cannot look into the heart; but your charitable feelings might well have refrained from awakening such a suspicion as mine.

ARSINOÉ.   Nothing is easier than to say no more about it, if you do not wish to be undeceived.

ALCESTE.   Just so. But whatever may be openly said on this subject is not half so annoying as hints thrown out; and I for one would prefer to be plainly told that only which could be clearly proved.

ARSINOÉ.   Very well! and that is sufficient; I can fully enlighten you upon this subject. I will have you believe nothing but what your own eyes see. Only have the kindness to escort me as far as my house; and I will give you undeniable proof of the faithlessness of your fair one's heart; and if, after that, you can find charms in anyone else, we will perhaps find you some consolation.

ACT IV.

SCENE I.

ÉLIANTE, PHILINTE.

PHILINTE. No, never have I seen so obstinate a mind, nor a reconciliation more difficult to effect. In vain was Alceste tried on all sides; he would still maintain his opinion; and never, I believe, has a more curious dispute engaged the attention of those gentlemen. "No, gentlemen," exclaimed he, "I will not retract, and I shall agree with you on every point, except on this one. At what is Oronte offended? and with what does he reproach me? Does it reflect upon his honor that he cannot write well? What is my opinion to him, which he has altogether wrongly construed? One may be a perfect gentleman, and write bad verses; those things have nothing to do with honor. I take him to be a gallant man in every way; a man of standing, of merit, and courage, anything you like, but he is a wretched author. I shall praise, if you wish, his mode of living, his lavishness, his skill in riding, in fencing, in dancing; but as to praising his verses, I am his humble servant; and if one has not the gift of composing better, one ought to leave off rhyming altogether, unless condemned to it on forfeit of one's life." In short, all the modification they could with difficulty obtain from him, was to say, in what he thought a much gentler tone—"I am sorry, sir, to be so difficult to please; and out of regard to you, I could wish, with all my heart, to have found your sonnet a little better." And they compelled them to settle this dispute quickly with an embrace.

ÉLIANTE. He is very eccentric in his doings; but I must confess that I think a great deal of him; and the candor upon which he prides himself has something noble and heroic in it. It is a rare virtue now-a-days, and I, for one, should not be sorry to meet with it everywhere.

PHILINTE.   As for me, the more I see of him, the more I am amazed at that passion to which his whole heart is given up. I cannot conceive how, with a disposition like his, he has taken it into his head to love at all; and still less can I understand how your cousin happens to be the person to whom his feelings are inclined.

ÉLIANTE.   That shows that love is not always produced by compatibility of temper; and in this case, all the pretty theories of gentle sympathies are belied.

PHILINTE.   But do you think him beloved in return, to judge from what we see?

ÉLIANTE.   That is a point not easily decided. How can we judge whether it be true she loves? Her own heart is not so very sure of what it feels. It sometimes loves, without being quite aware of it, and at other times thinks it does, without the least grounds.

PHILINTE.   I think that our friend will have more trouble with this cousin of yours than he imagines; and to tell you the truth, if he were of my mind, he would bestow his affections elsewhere; and by a better choice, we should see him, Madam, profit by the kind feelings which your heart evinces for him.

ÉLIANTE.   As for me, I do not mince matters, and I think that in such cases we ought to act with sincerity. I do not run counter to his tender feelings; on the contrary, I feel interested in them; and, if it depended only on me, I would unite him to the object of his love. But if, as it may happen in love affairs, his affections should receive a check, and if Célimène should respond to the love of any one else, I could easily be prevailed upon to listen to his addresses, and I should have no repugnance whatever to them on account of their rebuff elsewhere.

PHILINTE.   Nor do I, from my side, oppose myself, Madam, to the tender feelings which you entertain for him; and he himself, if he wished, could inform you what I have taken care to say to him on that score. But if, by the union of those two, you should be prevented from accepting his attentions, all mine would endeavor to gain that great favor which your kind feelings offer to him; only too happy, Madam, to have them transferred to myself, if his heart could not respond to yours.

ÉLIANTE.   You are in the humor to jest, Philinte.

PHILINTE.   Not so, Madam, I am speaking my inmost feelings. I only wait the opportune moment to offer myself openly, and am wishing most anxiously to hurry its advent.

SCENE II.

ALCESTE, ÉLIANTE, PHILINTE.

ALCESTE.   Ah, Madam! obtain me justice, for an offence which triumphs over all my constancy.

ÉLIANTE.   What ails you? What disturbs you?

ALCESTE.   This much ails me, that it is death to me to think of it; and the upheaving of all creation would less overwhelm me than this accident. It is all over with me . . . My love . . . I cannot speak.

ÉLIANTE.   Just endeavor to be composed.

ALCESTE.   Oh, just Heaven; can the odious vices of the basest minds be joined to such beauty?

ÉLIANTE.   But, once more, what can have . . .

ALCESTE.   Alas! All is ruined! I am! I am betrayed! I am stricken to death. Célimène . . . would you credit it! Célimène deceives me and is faithless.

ÉLIANTE.   Have you just grounds for believing so?

PHILINTE.   Perhaps it is a suspicion, rashly conceived; and your jealous temper often harbors fancies . . .

ALCESTE.   Ah! 'Sdeath, please to mind your own business, sir. [To ÉLIANTE] Her treachery is but too certain, for I have in my pocket a letter in her own handwriting. Yes, Madam, a letter, intended for Oronte, has placed before my eyes my disgrace and her shame; Oronte, whose addresses I believed she avoided, and whom, of all my rivals, I feared the least.

PHILINTE.   A letter may deceive by appearances, and is sometimes not so culpable as may be thought.

ALCESTE.   Once more, sir, leave me alone, if you please, and trouble yourself only about your own concerns.

ÉLIANTE.   You should moderate your passion; and the insult . . .

ALCESTE.   You must be left to do that, Madam; it is to you that my heart has recourse to-day to free itself from this goading pain. Avenge me on an ungrateful and perfidious relative who basely deceives such constant tenderness. Avenge me for an act that ought to fill you with horror.

ÉLIANTE.   I avenge you? How?

ALCESTE.   By accepting my heart. Take it, Madam, instead of the false

one; it is in this way that I can avenge myself upon her; and I shall
punish her by the sincere attachment, and the profound love, the
respectful cares, the eager devotions, the ceaseless attentions which
this heart will henceforth offer up at your shrine.

ÉLIANTE.   I certainly sympathize with you in your sufferings, and do
not despise your proffered heart; but the wrong done may not be so
great as you think, and you might wish to forego this desire for
revenge. When the injury proceeds from a beloved object, we form
many designs which we never execute; we may find as powerful a
reason as we like to break off the connection, the guilty charmer is
soon again innocent; all the harm we wish her quickly vanishes, and
we know what a lover's anger means.

ALCESTE.   No, no, Madam, no. The offence is too cruel; there will be
no relenting, and I have done with her. Nothing shall change the
resolution I have taken, and I should hate myself for ever loving her
again. Here she comes. My anger increases at her approach. I shall
taunt her with her black guilt, completely put her to the blush, and,
after that, bring you a heart wholly freed from her deceitful attractions.

SCENE III.

CÉLIMÈNE, ALCESTE.

ALCESTE.   [*Aside*] Grant, Heaven, that I may control my temper.

CÉLIMÈNE.   [*Aside*] Ah! [*To* ALCESTE] What is all this trouble that I see
you in, and what means those long-drawn sighs, and those black looks
which you cast at me?

ALCESTE.   That all the wickedness of which a heart is capable is not to
be compared to your perfidy; that neither fate, hell, nor Heaven in its
wrath, ever produced anything so wicked as you are.

CÉLIMÈNE.   These are certainly pretty compliments, which I admire
very much.

ALCESTE.   Do not jest. This is no time for laughing. Blush rather, you
have cause to do so; and I have undeniable proofs of your treachery.
This is what the agitations of my mind prognosticated; it was not
without cause that my love took alarm; by these frequent suspicions,
which were hateful to you, I was trying to discover the misfortune

which my eyes have beheld; and in spite of all your care and your skill in dissembling, my star foretold me what I had to fear. But do not imagine that I will bear unavenged this slight of being insulted. I know that we have no command over our inclinations, that love will every-where spring up spontaneously, that there is no entering a heart by force, and that every soul is free to name its conqueror: I should thus have no reason to complain if you had spoken to me without dissem-bling, and rejected my advances from the very beginning; my heart would then have been justified in blaming fortune alone. But to see my love encouraged by a deceitful avowal on your part, is an action so treacherous and perfidious, that it cannot meet with too great a punish-ment; and I can allow my resentment to do anything. Yes, yes; after such an outrage, fear everything; I am no longer myself, I am mad with rage. My senses, struck by the deadly blow with which you kill me, are no longer governed by reason; I give way to the outbursts of a just wrath, and am no longer responsible for what I may do.

CÉLIMÈNE.   Whence comes, I pray, such a passion? Speak! Have you lost your senses?

ALCESTE.   Yes, yes, I lost them when, to my misfortune, I beheld you and thus took the poison which kills me, and when I thought to meet with some sincerity in those treacherous charms that bewitched me.

CÉLIMÈNE.   Of what treachery have you to complain?

ALCESTE.   Ah! how double-faced she is! how well she knows how to dissemble! But I am fully prepared with the means of driving her to extremities. Cast your eyes here and recognize your writing. This picked-up note is sufficient to confound you, and such proof cannot easily be refuted.

CÉLIMÈNE.   And this is the cause of your perturbation of spirits?

ALCESTE.   You do not blush on beholding this writing!

CÉLIMÈNE.   And why should I blush?

ALCESTE.   What! You add boldness to craft! Will you disown this note because it bears no name?

CÉLIMÈNE.   Why should I disown it, since I wrote it?

ALCESTE.   And you can look at it without becoming confused at the crime of which its style accuses you!

CÉLIMÈNE.   You are, in truth, a very eccentric man.

ALCESTE.   What! You thus out-brave this convincing proof! And the contents so full of tenderness for Oronte, need have nothing in them to outrage me, or to shame you?

CÉLIMÈNE.   Oronte! Who told you that this letter is for him?

ALCESTE.   The people who put it into my hands this day. But I will even suppose that it is for some one else. Has my heart any less cause to complain of yours? Will you, in fact, be less guilty towards me?

CÉLIMÈNE.   But if it is a woman to whom this letter is addressed, how can it hurt you, or what is there culpable in it?

ALCESTE.   Hem! The prevarication is ingenious, and the excuse excellent. I must own that I did not expect this turn; and nothing but that was wanting to convince me. Do you dare to have recourse to such palpable tricks? Do you think people entirely destitute of common sense? Come, let us see a little by what subterfuge, with what air, you will support so palpable a falsehood; and how you can apply to a woman every word of this note which evinces so much tenderness! Reconcile, if you can, to hide your deceit, what I am about to read . . .

CÉLIMÈNE.   It does not suit me to do so. I think it ridiculous that you should take so much upon yourself, and tell me to my face what you have the daring to say to me!

ALCESTE.   No, no, without flying into a rage, take a little trouble to explain these terms.

CÉLIMÈNE.   No, I shall do nothing of the kind, and it matters very little to me what you think upon the subject.

ALCESTE.   I pray you, show me, and I shall be satisfied, if this letter can be explained as meant for a woman.

CÉLIMÈNE.   Not at all. It is for Oronte; and I will have you believe it. I accept all his attentions gladly; I admire what he says, I like him, and I shall agree to whatever you please. Do as you like, and act as you think proper; let nothing hinder you and do not harass me any longer.

ALCESTE.   [*Aside*] Heavens! can anything more cruel be conceived, and was ever heart treated like mine? What! I am justly angry with her, I come to complain, and I am quarreled with instead! My grief and my suspicions are excited to the utmost, I am allowed to believe everything, she boasts of everything; and yet, my heart is still sufficiently mean not to be able to break the bonds that hold it fast, and not to arm itself with a generous contempt for the ungrateful object of which it is too much enamored. [*To* CÉLIMÈNE] Perfidious woman, you know well how to take advantage of my great weakness, and to employ for your own purpose that excessive, astonishing, and fatal love which your treacherous looks have inspired! Defend yourself at least from this crime that overwhelms me, and stop pretending to be guilty. Show me, if you can, that this letter is innocent; my affection will even consent to assist you. At any rate, endeavor to appear faithful, and I shall strive to believe you such.

CÉLIMÈNE.   Bah, you are mad with your jealous frenzies, and do not deserve the love which I have for you. I should much like to know what could compel me to stoop for you to the baseness of dissembling; and why, if my heart were disposed towards another, I should not say so candidly. What! does the kind assurance of my sentiments towards you not defend me sufficiently against all your suspicions? Ought they to possess any weight at all with such a guarantee? Is it not insulting me even to listen to them? And since it is with the utmost difficulty that we can resolve to confess our love, since the strict honor of our sex, hostile to our passion, strongly opposes such a confession, ought a lover who sees such an obstacle overcome for his sake, doubt with impunity our avowal? And is he not greatly to blame in not assuring himself of the truth of that which is never said but after a severe struggle with one's self? Begone, such suspicions deserve my anger, and you are not worthy of being cared for. I am silly, and am vexed at my own simplicity in still preserving the least kindness for you. I ought to place my affections elsewhere, and give you a just cause for complaint.

ALCESTE.   Ah! you traitress! mine is a strange infatuation for you; those tender expressions are, no doubt, meant only to deceive me. But it matters little, I must submit to my fate; my very soul is wrapt up in you; I will see to the bitter end how your heart will act towards me, and whether it will be black enough to deceive me.

CÉLIMÈNE.   No, you do not love me as you ought to love.

ALCESTE.   Indeed! Nothing is to be compared to my exceeding love; and, in its eagerness to show itself to the whole world, it goes even so far as to form wishes against you. Yes, I could wish that no one thought you handsome, that you were reduced to a miserable existence; that Heaven, at your birth, had bestowed upon you nothing; that you had no rank, no nobility, no wealth, so that I might openly proffer my heart, and thus make amends to you for the injustice of such a lot; and that, this very day, I might have the joy and the glory of seeing you owe everything to my love.

CÉLIMÈNE.   This is wishing me well in a strange way! Heaven grant that you may never have occasion . . . But here comes Monsieur Dubois curiously decked out.

SCENE IV.

CÉLIMÈNE, ALCESTE, DUBOIS.

ALCESTE. What means this strange attire, and that frightened look? What ails you?
DUBOIS. Sir . . .
ALCESTE. Well?
DUBOIS. The most mysterious event.
ALCESTE. What is it?
DUBOIS. Our affairs are turning out badly, sir.
ALCESTE. What?
DUBOIS. Shall I speak out?
ALCESTE. Yes, do, and quickly.
DUBOIS. Is there no one there?
ALCESTE. Curse your trifling! Will you speak?
DUBOIS. Sir, we must beat a retreat.
ALCESTE. What do you mean?
DUBOIS. We must steal away from this quietly.
ALCESTE. And why?
DUBOIS. I tell you that we must leave this place.
ALCESTE. The reason?
DUBOIS. You must go, sir, without staying to take leave.
ALCESTE. But what is the meaning of this strain?
DUBOIS. The meaning is, sir, that you must make yourself scarce.
ALCESTE. I shall knock you on the head to a certainty, booby, if you do not explain yourself more clearly.
DUBOIS. A fellow, sir, with a black dress, and as black a look, got as far as the kitchen to leave a paper with us, scribbled over in such a fashion that Old Nick himself could not have read it. It is about your law-suit, I make no doubt; but the very devil, I believe, could not make head nor tail of it.
ALCESTE. Well! what then? What has the paper to do with the going away of which you speak, you scoundrel?
DUBOIS. I must tell you, sir, that, about an hour afterwards, a gentleman who often calls, came to ask for you quite eagerly, and not finding you at home, quietly told me, knowing how attached I am to you, to let you know . . . Stop a moment, what the deuce is his name?

ALCESTE.   Never mind his name, you scoundrel, and tell me what he told you.

DUBOIS.   He is one of your friends, in short, that is sufficient. He told me that for your very life you must get away from this, and that you are threatened with arrest.

ALCESTE.   But how! has he not specified anything?

DUBOIS.   No. He asked me for ink and paper, and has sent you a line from which you can, I think, fathom the mystery!

ALCESTE.   Hand it over then.

CÉLIMÈNE.   What can all this mean?

ALCESTE.   I do not know; but I am anxious to be informed. Have you almost done, devil take you?

DUBOIS.   [*After having fumbled for some time for the note*] After all, sir, I have left it on your table.

ALCESTE.   I do not know what keeps me from . . .

CÉLIMÈNE.   Do not put yourself in a passion, but go and unravel this perplexing business.

ALCESTE.   It seems that fate, whatever I may do, has sworn to prevent my having a conversation with you. But, to get the better of her, allow me to see you again, Madam, before the end of the day.

ACT V.

SCENE I.

ALCESTE, PHILINTE.

ALCESTE. I tell you, my mind is made up about it.

PHILINTE. But, whatever this blow may be, does it compel you . . .

ALCESTE. You may talk and argue till doomsday if you like, nothing can avert me from what I have said. The age we live in is too perverse, and I am determined to withdraw altogether from intercourse with the world. What! when honor, probity, decency, and the laws are all against my adversary; when the equity of my claim is everywhere cried up; when my mind is at rest as to the justice of my cause, I meanwhile see myself betrayed by its issue! What! I have got justice on my side, and I lose my case! A wretch, whose scandalous history is well known, comes off triumphant by the blackest falsehood! All good faith yields to his treachery! He finds the means of being in the right, whilst cutting my throat! The weight of his dissimulation, so full of cunning, over-throws the right and turns the scales of justice! He obtains even a decree of court to crown his villainy. And, not content with the wrong he is doing me, there is abroad in society an abominable book, of which the very reading is to be condemned, a book that deserves the utmost severity, and of which the scoundrel has the impudence to proclaim me the author. Upon this, Oronte is observed to mutter, and tries wickedly to support the imposture! He, who holds an honorable position at court, to whom I have done nothing without having been sincere and candid, who came to ask me in spite of myself of my opinion of some of his verses; and because I treat him honestly, and will not betray either him or truth, he assists in overwhelming me with a trumped-up crime. Behold him now my greatest enemy! And I shall never obtain his sincere forgiveness, because I did not think that his

43

sonnet was good! 'Sdeath! to think that mankind is made thus! The thirst for fame induces them to do such things! This is the good faith, the virtuous zeal, the justice and the honor to be found amongst them! Let us begone; it is too much to endure the vexations they are devising; let us get out of this wood, this cut-throat hole; and since men behave towards each other like real wolves, wretches, you shall never see me again as long as I live.

PHILINTE.   I think you are acting somewhat hastily; and the harm done is not so great as you would make it out. Whatever your adversary dares to impute to you has not had the effect of causing you to be arrested. We see his false reports defeating themselves, and this action is likely to hurt him much more than you.

ALCESTE.   Him? he does not mind the scandal of such tricks as these. He has a license to be an arrant knave; and this event, far from damaging his position, will obtain him a still better standing to-morrow.

PHILINTE.   In short, it is certain that little notice has been taken of the report which his malice spread against you; from that side you have already nothing to fear; and as for your law-suit, of which you certainly have reason to complain, it is easy for you to bring the trial on afresh, and against this decision . . .

ALCESTE.   No, I shall leave it as it is. Whatever cruel wrong this verdict may inflict, I shall take particular care not to have it set aside. We see too plainly how right is maltreated in it, and I wish to go down to posterity as a signal proof, as a notorious testimony of the wickedness of the men of our age. It may indeed cost me twenty thousand francs, but at the cost of twenty thousand francs I shall have the right of railing against the iniquity of human nature, and of nourishing an undying hatred of it.

PHILINTE.   But after all . . .

ALCESTE.   But after all, your pains are thrown away. What can you, sir, say upon this head? Would you have the assurance to wish, to my face, to excuse the villainy of all that is happening?

PHILINTE.   No, I agree with you in all that you say. Everything goes by intrigue, and by pure influence. It is only trickery which carries the day in our time, and men ought to act differently. But is their want of equity a reason for wishing to withdraw from their society? All human failings give us, in life, the means of exercising our philosophy. It is the best employment for virtue; and if probity reigned everywhere, if all hearts were candid, just, and tractable, most of our virtues would be useless to us, inasmuch as their functions are to bear, without annoyance, the injustice of others in our good cause; and just in the same way as a heart full of virtue . . .

ALCESTE. I know that you are a most fluent speaker, sir; that you always abound in fine arguments; but you are wasting your time, and all your fine speeches. Reason tells me to retire for my own good. I cannot command my tongue sufficiently; I cannot answer for what I might say, and should very probably get myself into a hundred scrapes. Allow me, without any more words, to wait for Célimène. She must consent to the plan that brings me here. I shall see whether her heart has any love for me; and this very hour will prove it to me.

PHILINTE. Let us go upstairs to Éliante, and wait her coming.

ALCESTE. No, my mind is too harassed. You go and see her, and leave me in this little dark corner with my black care.

PHILINTE. That is strange company to leave you in; I will induce Éliante to come down.

SCENE II.

CÉLIMÈNE, ORONTE, ALCESTE.

ORONTE. Yes, Madam, it remains for you to consider whether, by ties so dear, you will make me wholly yours. I must be absolutely certain of your affection: A lover dislikes to be held in suspense upon such a subject. If the ardor of my affection has been able to move your feelings, you ought not to hesitate to let me see it; and the proof, after all, which I ask of you, is not to allow Alceste to wait upon you any longer; to sacrifice him to my love, and, in short, to banish him from your house this very day.

CÉLIMÈNE. But why are you so incensed against him; you, whom I have so often heard speak of his merits?

ORONTE. There is no need, Madam, of these explanations; the question is, what are your feelings? Please to choose between the one or the other; my resolution depends entirely upon yours.

ALCESTE. [Coming out of his corner] Yes, this gentleman is right, Madam, you must make a choice; and his request agrees perfectly with mine. I am equally eager, and the same anxiety brings me here. My love requires a sure proof. Things cannot go on any longer in this way, and the moment has arrived for explaining your feelings.

ORONTE. I have no wish, sir, in any way to disturb, by an untimely affection, your good fortune.

ALCESTE. And I have no wish, sir, jealous or not jealous, to share aught in her heart with you.

ORONTE. If she prefers your affection to mine . . .

ALCESTE. If she has the slightest inclination towards you . . .

ORONTE. I swear henceforth not to pretend to it again.

ALCESTE. I peremptorily swear never to see her again.

ORONTE. Madam, it remains with you now to speak openly.

ALCESTE. Madam, you can explain yourself fearlessly.

ORONTE. You have simply to tell us where your feelings are engaged.

ALCESTE. You may simply finish the matter, by choosing between us two.

ORONTE. What! you seem to be at a loss to make such a choice.

ALCESTE. What! your heart still wavers, and appears uncertain!

CÉLIMÈNE. Good Heavens, how out of place is this persistence, and how very unreasonable you both show yourselves! It is not that I do not know whom to prefer, nor is it my heart that wavers. It is not at all in doubt between you two; and nothing could be more quickly accomplished than the choice of my affections. But to tell the truth, I feel too confused to pronounce such an avowal before you; I think that disobliging words ought not to be spoken in people's presence; that a heart can give sufficient proof of its attachment without going so far as to break with everyone; and gentler intimations suffice to inform a lover of the ill success of his suit.

ORONTE. No, no, I do not fear a frank avowal; for my part I consent to it.

ALCESTE. And I demand it; it is just its very publicity that I claim, and I do not wish you to spare my feelings in the least. Your great study has always been to keep friends with everyone; but no more trifling, no more uncertainty. You must explain yourself clearly, or I shall take your refusal as a verdict; I shall know, for my part, how to interpret your silence, and shall consider it as a confirmation of the worst.

ORONTE. I owe you many thanks, sir, for this wrath, and I say in every respect as you do.

CÉLIMÈNE.   How you weary me with such a whim! Is there any justice in what you ask? And have I not told you what motive prevents me? I will be judged by Éliante, who is just coming.

SCENE III.

ÉLIANTE, PHILINTE, CÉLIMÈNE, ORONTE, ALCESTE.

CÉLIMÈNE.   Good cousin, I am being persecuted here by people who have concerted to do so. They both demand, with the same warmth, that I should declare whom my heart has chosen, and that, by a decision which I must give before their very faces, I should forbid one of them to tease me any more with his attentions. Say, has ever such a thing been done?
ÉLIANTE.   Pray, do not consult me upon such a matter. You may perhaps address yourself to a wrong person, for I am decidedly for people who speak their mind.
ORONTE.   Madam, it is useless for you to decline.
ALCESTE.   All your evasions here will be badly supported.
ORONTE.   You must speak, you must, and no longer waver.
ALCESTE.   You need do no more than remain silent.
ORONTE.   I desire but one word to end our discussions.
ALCESTE.   To me your silence will convey as much as speech.

SCENE IV.

ARSINOÉ, CÉLIMÈNE, ÉLIANTE, ALCESTE, PHILINTE, ACASTE, CLITANDRE, ORONTE.

ACASTE.   [To CÉLIMÈNE] We have both come, by your leave, Madam, to clear up a certain little matter with you.
CLITANDRE.   [To ORONTE and ALCESTE] Your presence happens fortunately, gentlemen; for this affair concerns you also.
ARSINOÉ.   [To CÉLIMÈNE] No doubt you are surprised at seeing me here, Madam; but these gentlemen are the cause of my intrusion. They both came to see me, and complained of a proceeding which I

could not have credited. I have too high an opinion of your kindness of heart ever to believe you capable of such a crime; my eyes even have refused to give credence to their strongest proofs, and in my friendship, forgetting trivial disagreements, I have been induced to accompany them here, to hear you refute this slander.

ACASTE.   Yes, Madam, let us see, with composure, how you will manage to bear this out. This letter has been written by you, to Clitandre.

CLITANDRE.   And this tender epistle you have addressed to Acaste.

ACASTE.   [*To* ORONTE *and* ALCESTE] This writing is not altogether unknown to you, gentlemen, and I have no doubt that her kindness has before now made you familiar with her hand. But this is well worth the trouble of reading.

> *"You are a strange man to condemn my liveliness of spirits, and to reproach me that I am never so merry as when I am not with you. Nothing could be more unjust; and if you do not come very soon to ask my pardon for this offence, I shall never forgive you as long as I live. Our great hulking booby of a Viscount . . ."* He ought to have been here. *"Our great hulking booby of a Viscount, with whom you begin your complaints, is a man who would not at all suit me; and ever since I watched him for full three-quarters of an hour spitting in a well to make circles in the water, I never could have a good opinion of him. As for the little Marquis . . ."* that is myself, ladies and gentlemen, be it said without the slightest vanity, . . . *"as for the little Marquis, who held my hand yesterday for a long while, I think that there is nothing so diminutive as his whole person, and his sole merit consists in his cloak and sword. As to the man with the green shoulder knot . . ."* [*To* ALCESTE] It is your turn now, sir. *"As to the man with the green shoulder knot, he amuses me sometimes with his bluntness and his splenetic behavior; but there are hundreds of times when I think him the greatest bore in the world. Respecting the man with the big waistcoat . . ."* [*To* ORONTE] This is your share. *"Respecting the man with the big waistcoat, who has thought fit to set up as a wit, and wishes to be an author in spite of everyone, I cannot even take the trouble to listen to what he says; and his prose bores me just as much as his poetry. Take it for granted that I do not always enjoy myself so much as you think; and that I wish for you, more than I care to say, amongst all the entertainments to which I am dragged; and that the presence of those we love is an excellent relish to our pleasures."*

CLITANDRE.   Now for myself.

"Your Clitandre, whom you mention to me, and who has always such a quantity of soft expressions at his command, is the last man for whom I could feel any affection. He must be crazed in persuading himself that I love him; and you are so too in believing that I do not love you. You had better change your fancies for his, and come and see me as often as you can, to help me in bearing the annoyance of being pestered by him."

This shows the model of a lovely character, Madam; and I need not tell you what to call it. It is enough. We shall, both of us, show this admirable sketch of your heart everywhere and to everybody.

ACASTE.   I might also say something, and the subject is tempting; but I deem you beneath my anger; and I will show you that little marquises can find worthier hearts than yours to console themselves.

SCENE V.

CÉLIMÈNE, ÉLIANTE, ARSINOÉ, ALCESTE, ORONTE, PHILINTE.

ORONTE.   What! Am I to be pulled to pieces in this fashion, after all that you have written to me? And does your heart, with all its semblance of love, plight its faith to all mankind by turns! Bah, I have been too great a dupe, but I shall be so no longer. You have done me a service, in showing yourself in your true colors to me. I am the richer by a heart which you thus restore to me, and find my revenge in your loss. [To ALCESTE] Sir, I shall no longer be an obstacle to your flame, and you may settle matters with this lady as soon as you please.

SCENE VI.

CÉLIMÈNE, ÉLIANTE, ARSINOÉ, ALCESTE, PHILINTE.

ARSINOÉ.   [To CÉLIMÈNE] This is certainly one of the basest actions which I have ever seen; I can no longer be silent, and feel quite upset.

Has any one ever seen the like of it? I do not concern myself much in the affairs of other people, but this gentleman [*pointing to* ALCESTE], who has staked the whole of his happiness on you, an honorable and deserving man like this, and who worshipped you to madness, ought he to have been . . .

ALCESTE. Leave me, I pray you, Madam, to manage my own affairs; and do not trouble yourself unnecessarily. In vain do I see you espouse my quarrel. I am unable to repay you for this great zeal; and if ever I intended to avenge myself by choosing some one else, it would not be you whom I would select.

ARSINOÉ. And do you imagine, sir, that I ever harbored such a thought, and that I am so very anxious to secure you? You must be very vain, indeed, to flatter yourself with such an idea. Célimène's leavings are a commodity, of which no one needs be so very much enamored. Pray, undeceive yourself, and do not carry matters with so high a hand. People like me are not for such as you. You will do much better to remain dangling after her skirts, and I long to see so beautiful a match.

SCENE VII.

CÉLIMÈNE, ÉLIANTE, ALCESTE, PHILINTE.

ALCESTE. [*To* CÉLIMÈNE] Well! I have held my tongue, notwithstanding all I have seen, and I have let everyone have his say before me. Have I controlled myself long enough? and will you now allow me . . .

CÉLIMÈNE. Yes, you may say what you like; you are justified when you complain, and you may reproach me with anything you please. I confess that I am in the wrong; and overwhelmed by confusion I do not seek by any idle excuse to palliate my fault. The anger of the others I have despised; but I admit my guilt towards you. No doubt, your resentment is just; I know how culpable I must appear to you, that everything speaks of my treachery to you and that, in short, you have cause to hate me. Do so, I consent to it.

ALCESTE. But can I do so, you traitress? Can I thus get the better of all my tenderness for you? And although I wish to hate you with all my soul, shall I find a heart quite ready to obey me? [*To* ÉLIANTE *and* PHILINTE] You see what an unworthy passion can do, and I call you both as witnesses of my infatuation. Nor, truth to say, is this all, and you will see me carry it out to the bitter end, to show you that it is wrong to call us wise, and that in all hearts there remains still something of the man. [*To* CÉLIMÈNE] Yes, perfidious creature, I am willing to forget your crimes. I can find, in my own heart, an excuse for all your doings, and hide them under the name of a weakness into which the vices of the age betrayed your youth, provided your heart will second the design which I have formed of avoiding all human creatures, and that you are determined to follow me without delay into the solitude in which I have made a vow to pass my days. It is by that only, that, in everyone's opinion, you can repair the harm done by your letters, and that, after the scandal which every noble heart must abhor, it may still be possible for me to love you.

CÉLIMÈNE.   What! I renounce the world before I grow old, and bury myself in your wilderness!

ALCESTE.   If your affection responds to mine what need the rest of the world signify to you? Am I not sufficient for you?

CÉLIMÈNE.   Solitude is frightful to a widow of twenty. I do not feel my mind sufficiently grand and strong to resolve to adopt such a plan. If the gift of my hand can satisfy your wishes, I might be induced to tie such bonds; and marriage . . .

ALCESTE.   No. My heart loathes you now, and this refusal alone effects more than all the rest. As you are not disposed, in those sweet ties, to find all in all in me, as I would find all in all in you, begone, I refuse your offer, and this much-felt outrage frees me for ever from your unworthy toils.

SCENE VIII.

ÉLIANTE, ALCESTE, PHILINTE.

ALCESTE.   [*To* ÉLIANTE] Madam, your beauty is adorned by a hundred virtues; and I never saw anything in you but what was sincere. For a long while I thought very highly of you; but allow me to esteem you thus for ever, and suffer my heart in its various troubles not to offer itself for the honor of your acceptance. I feel too unworthy, and begin to perceive that Heaven did not intend me for the marriage bond; that the homage of only the remainder of a heart unworthy of you would be below your merit, and that in short . . .

ÉLIANTE. You may pursue this thought. I am not at all embarrassed with my hand; and here is your friend, who, without giving me much trouble, might possibly accept it if I asked him.

PHILINTE. Ah! Madam, I ask for nothing better than that honor, and I could sacrifice my life and soul for it.

ALCESTE. May you, to taste true contentment, preserve for ever these feelings towards each other! Deceived on all sides, overwhelmed with injustice, I will fly from an abyss where vice is triumphant, and seek out some small secluded nook on earth, where one may enjoy the freedom of being an honest man.

PHILINTE. Come, Madam, let us leave nothing untried to deter him from the design on which his heart is set.

DOVER·THRIFT·EDITIONS

FICTION

FLATLAND: A ROMANCE OF MANY DIMENSIONS, Edwin A. Abbott. 96pp. 27263-X $1.00

PERSUASION, Jane Austen. 224pp. 29555-9 $2.00

PRIDE AND PREJUDICE, Jane Austen. 272pp. 28473-5 $2.00

SENSE AND SENSIBILITY, Jane Austen. 272pp. 29049-2 $2.00

WUTHERING HEIGHTS, Emily Brontë. 256pp. 29256-8 $2.00

BEOWULF, Beowulf (trans. by R. K. Gordon). 64pp. 27264-8 $1.00

CIVIL WAR STORIES, Ambrose Bierce. 128pp. 28038-1 $1.00

THE AUTOBIOGRAPHY OF AN EX-COLORED MAN, James Weldon Johnson. 112pp. 28512-X $1.00

TARZAN OF THE APES, Edgar Rice Burroughs. 224pp. (Available in U.S. only) 29570-2 $2.00

ALICE'S ADVENTURES IN WONDERLAND, Lewis Carroll. 96pp. 27543-4 $1.00

O PIONEERS!, Willa Cather. 128pp. 27785-2 $1.00

MY ÁNTONIA, Willa Cather. 176pp. 28240-6 $2.00

PAUL'S CASE AND OTHER STORIES, Willa Cather. 64pp. 29057-3 $1.00

IN A GERMAN PENSION: 13 Stories, Katherine Mansfield. 112pp. 28719-X $1.50

THE STORY OF AN AFRICAN FARM, Olive Schreiner. 256pp. 40165-0 $2.00

"THE YELLOW WALLPAPER" AND OTHER STORIES, Charlotte Perkins Gilman. 80pp. 29857-4 $1.00

HERLAND, Charlotte Perkins Gilman. 128pp. 40429-3 $1.50

FIVE GREAT SHORT STORIES, Anton Chekhov. 96pp. 26463-7 $1.00

"THE FIDDLER OF THE REELS" AND OTHER SHORT STORIES, Thomas Hardy. 80pp. 29960-0 $1.50

FAVORITE FATHER BROWN STORIES, G. K. Chesterton. 96pp. 27545-0 $1.00

THE WARDEN, Anthony Trollope. 176pp. 40076-X $2.00

THE COUNTRY OF THE POINTED FIRS, Sarah Orne Jewett. 96pp. 28196-5 $1.00

GREAT SHORT STORIES BY AMERICAN WOMEN, Candace Ward (ed.). 192pp. 28776-9 $2.00

SHORT STORIES, Louisa May Alcott. 64pp. 29063-8 $1.00

THE AWAKENING, Kate Chopin. 128pp. 27786-0 $1.00

A PAIR OF SILK STOCKINGS AND OTHER STORIES, Kate Chopin. 64pp. 29264-9 $1.00

THE REVOLT OF "MOTHER" AND OTHER STORIES, Mary E. Wilkins Freeman. 128pp. 40428-5 $1.50

HEART OF DARKNESS, Joseph Conrad. 80pp. 26464-5 $1.00

THE SECRET SHARER AND OTHER STORIES, Joseph Conrad. 128pp. 27546-9 $1.00

THE "LITTLE REGIMENT" AND OTHER CIVIL WAR STORIES, Stephen Crane. 80pp. 29557-5 $1.00

THE OPEN BOAT AND OTHER STORIES, Stephen Crane. 128pp. 27547-7 $1.50

THE RED BADGE OF COURAGE, Stephen Crane. 112pp. 26465-3 $1.00

A CHRISTMAS CAROL, Charles Dickens. 80pp. 26865-9 $1.00

THE CRICKET ON THE HEARTH AND OTHER CHRISTMAS STORIES, Charles Dickens. 128pp. 28039-X $1.00

THE DOUBLE, Fyodor Dostoyevsky. 128pp. 29572-9 $1.50

NOTES FROM THE UNDERGROUND, Fyodor Dostoyevsky. 96pp. 27053-X $1.00

THE GAMBLER, Fyodor Dostoyevsky. 112pp. 29081-6 $1.50

THE ADVENTURE OF THE DANCING MEN AND OTHER STORIES, Sir Arthur Conan Doyle. 80pp. 29558-3 $1.00

THE HOUND OF THE BASKERVILLES, Arthur Conan Doyle. 128pp. 28214-7 $1.00

SIX GREAT SHERLOCK HOLMES STORIES, Sir Arthur Conan Doyle. 112pp. 27055-6 $1.00

SILAS MARNER, George Eliot. 160pp. 29246-0 $1.50